Ooo Shiny! Volume 5
The Search for Shiny 4

J M Samland

Dyingstar Press LLC

Contents

An Actual Introduction

S hiny 1... Lots of holiday ideas. So I made a Holiday Edition. Which had some vampires. So I wrote one with vampires. And it had more werewolves. This one should be sci-fi!

...

It has more horror and ruminations regarding death.

I said it before, and I'll say it again. Staying "off target" is rather "on brand" for me.

Trigger warnings include: Graphic violence, suicide, grief. No animals are harmed.

First Log

With the last of the crew securely in statis, I am allowed to unseal the files outlining our mission. Words and diagrams float past me in sharp, neon-blue script. Even with another dozen PhDs, I wouldn't be able to make sense of the math, and I begin to wonder if it was invented for this mission. It wouldn't be the first time. They say Galileo invented calculus to explain the motion of heavenly bodies. Why not some new arm of mathematics to track entire planes of existence?

It sounds like science fiction. But then, I'm the last awake in a crew of forty, hurtling through space at relativistic speeds. Everything about my life would have been unfathomable to my ancestors a dozen generations back.

They may relate to what my life will be for the few months.

Complete solitude.

Yes, the AI is trained with a dozen personalities and can inhabit any of the drones to fulfill the needs of the ship or of me, but the fact that one of the crew must always be awake speaks volumes about the faith the engineers put in their invention.

Wow.

It feels great to say this out loud. To know that I am beyond the reach of humanity, yet am able to remark on their cruelty? That I couldn't have this voice while among the rest of my species? Every day on this ship, Earth does more than a full spin around the sun. By the time we reach maximum velocity, which will be just before the end of my first shift, I can't imagine humanity will still exist. Though if we ever manage to break the speed-of-light barrier, maybe they'll pick us up and abort this mission within a month.

Relativistic time is weird. Even after writing two of my dissertations on topics tangential to it, it's still different to live it.

Long story short, unless humans create technology to outrun us (and they don't forget about us) or we aren't found by another species, there is no return from this mission. The premise is insane: to find a lost reality. A reality no one was looking for. But I couldn't pass up the chance. I don't care about the mission goal, but this ship, with all its sleeping passengers and robust AI, is the closest thing I'll have to fast-forwarding through time. The present holds nothing for me, so I leave it behind, like the ion cloud trailing this vessel.

Meanwhile, my first shift begins. I'll play chess, study languages, and watch the telemetry that the AI can process infinitely faster than my flesh brain can. Three months later, while generations come and go on the planet we left behind, I'll wake the next traveler and slip into statis. When I wake again… I'm looking forward to swinging our telescope back at the blue fleck of dust and seeing how it's changed after a few thousand years.

Or maybe we'll find what we're tasked to find. I'm just here for the ride.

Boulangerie Fée

The new bakery on my level is amazing. Or so I hear. By the time I finish my shift and can get to it, the last muffin is long gone. Not even a slice of lemon pound cake remains. Yes, it's fae food, and the usual warning is not to eat fae food, but I'm sure that's a baseless warning from racist humans.

I've tried to get off early, to make it in time for a scone, but I'm still on the probationary period for this new job. Yeah, it's got health care, but I glossed over the fine print.

And there was a lot of fine print.

I might have expected that, taking a job with a rogue.

The sixteen-hour days are nice. A definite improvement over what I had at the last dungeon. But still, no time off yet.

I'm in my usual room with the other goblins, waiting for the party of "heroes" to enter and slay us. My recent promotion to Shaman Elite means I'm stationed in the back of the room, closer to the ogre lord boss. I survive longer than I used to, which means I can watch more of the fight before they get to me. I've already noticed a few things that the boss could implement to improve the room but I those will have to wait until my quarterly review.

I live longer, but I'm a healer and summoner class now, so most teams target me early.

Anyway, we're waiting for the next team... and waiting ...

A few goblins take out dice to pass the time. A few others pull paperback novels from their pouches. I wonder what the "heroes" think when they loot those off our corpses?

Finally, an announcement comes over the crackling loudspeaker.

"The dungeon is closed for maintenance. All sectors are offline until the next reset."

I've never heard of unplanned maintenance. Neither has anyone else, by the murmurs of confusion.

If all sectors are offline... That means I'm not expected to report elsewhere. Which means...

Still wearing my shaman robe and holding my summoning staff—I can get to the quartermaster soon enough—I rush from the ogre lord's lair. Past the spike traps and ambush sites and the lone healing well on the level, I arrive at Boulangerie Fée as every other goblin, ghoul, and masked bandit on the level had the same idea. A pair of skeletons ahead of me in line chatters about their excitement over their chance at a sweet treat today. They don't have a tongue or innards. How could they possibly enjoy a cinnamon bun?

Cookies and pastries are replaced with "SOLD OUT" signs as the line before me diminishes. No more honey buns. No more cake pops. No more hand pies or macarons. The skeletons buy the last sugar spirals.

At last, I'm looking up at the thin man in a sky-blue pantsuit and dandelion yellow cravat.

"I'll have one of anything!" I say, suddenly worried that more will be sold out if I take too long to order.

The man grins down at me, his mouth full of too many teeth. And that's saying something coming from a goblin.

"I have one goblin market sausage roll left. How's that sound, my little green friend?"

His magic washes over me. I would have bought anything he offered if not for the minor stat boost from my robes and staff. Even aware of his magical influence, I wasn't going to decline my first, and possibly only, chance to try something from the bakery.

I nod enthusiastically and dig through my coin purse while he wraps the sausage roll in crisp white paper.

Buttery pastry in hand, I step aside and lean my staff against a table. Taking a deep sniff of it, I can pick out each herb in a rapid progression, each making my mouth water more than the last. I want to draw it out, to enjoy this moment until my next shift starts at the next reset. This is my first time eating fae food, and I'll only have one first time.

"Yeah? You gonna eat meeee?"

I startle at the small, whispered voice drawing out syllables at random. No one is particularly near me, and no one seems to be paying me any mind.

"You want my buuuuuttery flakes? Yeah, you do."

"Hello?" I say to my goblin market sausage roll.

"It's chilly out here. Brrr. Better eat me while I'm the perrrrfect temperature."

With the last fig bar sold, the bakery is shutting down. Sad cyclopes and kobolds shuffle away while those who made it in time relish their treats at the tables and benches scattered across the lot.

"Are you... Are you alive?" I whisper

"No, silly. I'm a sauuuuusage roll. A juicy, meaty sausage roll. Bite into me and see the perfect laminaaaation of my buttery layers. Don't worry, I'm not made of goblin, as my name might implyyyy."

I do as it bids, taking a tiny nibble off the corner, and indeed, the layers are perfect.

"Does all the food from that bakery talk?"

"Only the ones that reeeeally want to be eaten. So yes. Come on, you big, strong goblin. Don't leave me waaaaaiting. Don't make me beeeeg."

I take a bigger bite. The meat and vegetables are immaculately balanced with the spices that hit every nerve in my mouth. The pastry casing melts to bliss.

"Yes! Don't linger too loooong! Swallow me down and finish me off!"

I want to ignore it, to savor this moment, but it would know the best way to eat itself.

I gobble down the rest in two bites, getting a bit of the paper wrapping it in the process.

The voice is gone, but I hear a hint of a contented sigh as I lick my fingers. Did it add anything to the experience? I likely would not have noticed the flaky lamination. Was it telling the truth that others would talk if you wait too long?

Well, all I know is that I'm now extra looking forward to the next unscheduled maintenance.

Double Haunt

My roommates complain that our old house is haunted. I don't know... I've been living here for over ninety years and haven't seen anything.

Har har. I kid. I'm dead and exist as a ghost. I am the haunt they complain about.

I guess that's probably pretty obvious. Cut me some slack, please. I don't have much chance to practice new material. Also, the premise of the joke is a lie. They don't notice me. I've never been able to interact much with the living in the house, other than the occasional spooky vibe. No rattling chains or moaning from the basement for me.

In the seventies, they got out a Ouija board and I tried really, really hard to participate. The young man only managed to scare his girlfriend, and they ran off from their friends, to another room, to kiss and other stuff. They didn't at all notice me jumping around the table and passing through it.

A physic medium came in both the forties and eighties. I waved and did a little dance for them, but they passed on. She said the house was clearly haunted, while staring right at, and through, me.

One of my roommates had a cat. I thought she was staring at me for two hours one night. The cat, not the roommate. It turns out there was a thumbtack in the wall that she thought was a bug.

It's been a lonely existence. I'm barely noticed, so no one's trying to resolve my unresolved business. I just watch them go about their lives, sometimes getting a flicker of joy when they complain about the room being cold.

I often read over their shoulders and clap with glee when they reach for a blanket, but I know how old and drafty the windows are.

My roommates right now... Okay, I can't keep calling the living my roommates. The people living in the house that I'm doing a bad job at haunting... They're having a fight. It's not uncommon for these two women to fight. They do it most nights. It's usually followed up by passionate moments in the bedroom. But not tonight.

They're in the workshop in the basement. I'm hanging out by the boiler. The blonde, Cher, says she's leaving. The dark-haired one, Lisa, says no way. Fight, fight, fight... Lisa has a pipe wrench in her hand...

Not that I'd ever be called as a witness in court, not in my present state, but it happened too fast for me to follow. The screaming stopped, or at least it changed from an argument to horror.

Cher is still screaming, but not in a way that Lisa can hear. She's hovering over her own body as Lisa stares at her shaking hands. The wrench clatters to the cement floor. Then, she shifts to cleaning up the scene. Lisa's eyes lock onto the boiler beside me, and I hope she does what I think she's going to do. That's one way to ensure that Cher stays on as my roommate for a while.

Cher stops screaming to watch Lisa open the cast-iron door and load her body into it. When she does, the darkness within calls to me, beckoning me to investigate. It's gone in a moment as she tosses the wrench in, locks the door, and cranks up the dial.

I've read enough Agatha Christy over people's shoulders to see the gaping flaws in her plans, but kudos to her for the quick thinking.

Lisa rushes upstairs, and Cher finally notices me. And starts screaming again.

"Who are you?" she manages.

I wave. "Hi. I'm Gordon. I'm a ghost."

Her mouth moves, searching for words, and she points between the pool of blood and the boiler.

I smile widely, hoping that I seem like pleasant company. "Yeah, you're a ghost too. It's not all that bad. And you won't be alone."

Cher approaches me, eyes narrowing. "Have you been here the whole time?"

Lisa is talking loudly on the phone upstairs. I can pick out phrases implying an unplanned trip with her and Cher.

"For almost a century, yeah. I think I might be in the boiler, actually. I felt weird when Lisa opened the door."

"You know our names? So were you watching us?"

Cher is close now, but I can't understand her expression.

"Sure," I shrug. "There's not much to do as a ghost."

"You pervert!" She shoves me, but other than an odd chilly feeling in my chest, her hands pass through me.

I raise my hands defensively. "No! Not like that! I didn't do anything creepy. I stepped out if... if things... I never... My momma raised me to be a gentleman."

"Yeah, I'm sure she did. Momma's boy. Where did Lisa go, Pervert?"

"Gordon. She's upstairs, planning her escape while your body incinerates."

Cher scoffs. "That's such a Lisa thing to do. Running as soon as things get hard."

"You're taking this rather well. Being murdered, that is."

She sighs. "I think I always knew she had it in her. Something about her eyes. I'm not going to lie. It's kind of hot that she actually did it. How did she look with her face splattered with my blood?"

"I, uh…"

"I wonder if she'll get away with it. I bet she will. You know she has an Italian passport? She's been threatening to use it to leave me."

"That would be a shame."

Cher squints at the boiler's dial. "Yeah, she's going to crank it up to a hundred in here and go to the cabin so she doesn't have to smell me bar-b-qeuing. Then she'll dump my bones in the woods and move to Rome." She's tracing a fingertip on her lips, engrossed in her own story.

"I wonder if that'll make you haunt the woods, then? What if she misses a few bones? I still don't know a lot about being a ghost." I say.

She pushes past me, going out of her way to shoulder check me on the way to the stairs. "Move it, Pervert."

My first conversation in almost a century…

Maybe it was better when the roommates ignored me.

Bit Late

I'm on the edge of the couch, only breathing when I remember to do it manually. A continuous stream of curses flow from my lips. I can't blink. Sixty-two hours of intense combat and diligent exploration have brought me to this moment. I know her movements, timed to the width of a hair. Still, I'm down to a sliver of life. But, so is she.

The doorbell rings, and Maribel loses her shit. She doesn't get up from her bed in the corner, but lets everyone know she's present, ready to defend the house as needed.

I miss a button and die. Cleaved in twain by the Valkyrie Queen.

Grumbling through the loading screen as I respawn, I push up and rip open the door.

The man in khaki shorts and a buttoned top looks as surprised to see me as I am him.

"Package for ya," he says, pointing to the box on the porch between us.

"Thanks," I say, but he's already back in his truck and moving off before I stand.

It's heavy with a lot of loose pieces sloshing around inside. Great. I wasn't expecting a delivery, and what I got is broken.

Maribel follows my movements into the kitchen, but doesn't get up. I cut the box open and within… Legos. Tons of loose bricks and a few assembly instruction booklets buried within.

No card. No note. No invoice or order slip. Just Legos from an unknown sender.

I can look up the tracking number later to see where it came from, but first, a Valkyrie Queen needs to die.

I align the runes to activate the bridge to her platform, sit through the four minutes of unskippable dialog and am about to engage again…

Except, there's another ring of the doorbell.

Maribel grumbles and puts her head down.

A man is standing on my porch, wearing a sky-blue pantsuit and a bright yellow cravat. Beside him stands a pony.

I manage, "What…?"

"Sorry, love. Some things take a while," he says in a comically intense Australian accent.

"Things? What things? Why do you have a pony?"

It considers me with one baleful eye. The other is covered by its shaggy, white mane.

"I just need you to sign here," he says, producing a clipboard.

"Sign for what?"

"Why, the pony, naturally."

His van is parked on the street. A normal delivery sprinter van. Not something one would use to transport a pony. "Feyland Wish Service, LLC" is printed in rainbow block letters over the mural as bright as his cravat.

"Wish service?" I say, stunned.

"Yeah, love. Again, sorry for the delay. Could you sign here for me?" He urges forward with the clipboard.

Wish service? What does that...

By van's the wheel well, the mural shows a kid blowing out candles on a birthday cake. A memory slams back, long hidden but now as clear as if it were yesterday.

My ninth birthday. I wanted Legos, because of course I did.

I wanted a pony. Not because I wanted to care for it, but because Uncle Eldon promised to take me to the petting zoo the following week.

Except Uncle Eldon wasn't there.

As a kid, I didn't know how sick he'd been for so long, or how brave he was for not allowing it to ruin his spirit.

So there I was, hovering over the cake, surrounded by cousins, wishing for Legos, but feeling the recent absence of my beloved uncle. I wanted the pony he promised me.

I *wished* for it.

Feyland Wish Service, LLC.

Oh no...

I'd wished for a third thing fourteen years ago...

"I have other deliveries, love," says the man in blue.

"I— sure, yeah, leave it around back." I scribble on the line at the bottom of the clipboard and slam the door before he can say another word. I jump into my shoes, tell Maribel to be good, grab a shovel, and am backing out of the garage as the man in blue is returning to his van.

I'll deal with the pony later. If two out of three wishes come true back-to-back, I have a very real feeling that something terrible is happening at Glenview Memorial Gardens.

Moon Cheese

There are a thousand written rules regarding the proper way to handle extra-Earth samples after they splash down and are brought back to the lab for testing. Some would argue that there are ten times as many more rules that are so obvious, no one should need to write them down.

But this is the first sample I've ever seen from the dark side of the moon.

And it really looks and smells like cheese.

And I really want to eat it.

Just a tiny nibble. It's traveled almost four hundred thousand kilometers to sit on a dish on the table in front of me. I only had so much. The sample was divided and distributed to two dozen laboratories across the globe. It's not like I could eat it all and ask for seconds.

I wouldn't be the first person to eat something for scie nce...

In 1951, the Explorer's Club claimed to serve a dinner of woolly mammoth. What a unique culinary delight! When would anyone ever again get the opportunity to eat a creature dead for thousands of years before the druids erected Stonehenge?

It turned out to be sea turtle meat.

In the early 70s, Géologie Fascinante in Southern France held an expo encouraging attendees to lick geological samples and record their opinions. That was, admittedly, more a thin excuse to lick rocks, rather than hard science.

In 2023, a company inserted woolly mammoth DNA into a sheep, but no one ate it. They were concerned about what ancient proteins would do to modern physiology. I can understand that a bit, but would one little tiny nibble have hurt that much?

But this isn't a woolly mammoth. This is cheese from the dark side of the moon. A sample that looks and smells and, as I poke it with tweezers, sure feels like feta. Twenty grams of delicious, soft feta.

As a lunar geologist, I could give a TED Talk, without prep, on how harsh the moon's environment is. Nothing "soft" exists there. With no wind or water to wear down the edges, every rock or flake of dust may as well be one of those Ginsu knives they used to have on late-night TV.

I check the manifest and chain of custody again, ensuring it's impossible that someone accidentally swapped the topping from the lunch's Greek salad with a sample from a hundred-million-dollar space mission.

Nope. Everything checks out.

This is a rock from the moon.

And it's cheese.

At least, I sure think it's cheese.

Maybe just a little nibble...

Second Log

I'd been put in statis during my training, but never for this long. Almost nine years.

Since I woke up my replacement and went to sleep, two of my colleagues had perished. One from a failed statis chamber, the other... Well, the AI wouldn't give me a solid explanation. The other was involved in some airlock mishap. The explosive decompression of Airlock Beta-2 altered our course, but the AI readjusted and recalculated a billion times since.

It took close to a week to feel "right" again after waking up. By my quick calculation, something like two thousand years had passed on Earth. I guess that means they either forgot about us, or humanity never developed faster-than-light travel.

More likely, one of the many malignant narcissists in charge of a country with nukes decided to leave their legacy. I'll run back the monitors still focused that way later to see what happened.

Should I be concerned that I don't care enough right now to rush to check?

There are thirty-eight of us left. There have been more than fifty exciting blips in the sensors, implying that what we were sent out to find does indeed exist, and we are still on the correct route to intersect it. The AI seems to know what that something is, though it won't tell me more, so I have to stick with the "search for a lost reality" mission briefing.

The ship has changed in the last nine years. New art installations in the open areas and a pile of freshly penned books in the rec room. My colleagues have been busy. I studied the art from every angle and plan to read the books as time allows. Even out in the nowhere between the stars, where the last surviving humans take turns being awake, we can't stop creating. Only the forty... thirty-eight... of us will ever see or read these creations, yet we keep going.

It kind of makes me want to try my hand at sketching...

But first, the AI has a list of tasks for me.

Cleaning out the food replicator and flushing the air filtration fluid.

I thought the AI was supposed to take care of all this.

It won't take long, then I'll get to reading.

Stay at Home

She used to kiss me before leaving for work. Now she doesn't look at me.

At least not often.

When I catch her doing it, she looks away. Tears in her eyes.

I read a book years ago that warned that once the kids move out, parents are hit hard. I get it. Our lives were nothing but Mark and Joey. Now Mark's abroad in London, and Joey moved in with his partner. Sandra and I are... different. We have to rediscover how to fill the time that the boys have taken up for the last two decades.

"I don't know how much longer I can keep this up," she said at dinner, speaking to her meatloaf. The table was empty in front of me. I haven't had much of an appetite for years.

Not since the accident.

"What do you mean?" I asked.

"I mean…" Her eyes flitted over me for an instant and settled on the globe light hanging over the table. She squeezed her eyes tight. "You know what I mean." Her jaw tensed, and the tears started.

I wanted to go to her, to comfort her, but I remained in my seat. Maybe this is what she meant? I had been distant. I knew this, but as aware as I was, I couldn't seem to get back to my old self. It wasn't easy to remember what that meant anymore.

Rather than standing, I looked down at the dog staring up at me expectantly.

"This has to end," she said, forcing the words, but I could see how much it hurt her.

Yet I remained in my seat.

"We have to say goodbye."

That got me to lean forward. "No, Sandra. No. I love you."

"I know." She finally brought her gaze to meet mine. "And I love you, Lyn. The boys love you. But… Do you remember when you last left the house?"

Heat and pain and shattering glass exploded across my memory, and were gone just as quickly. I shook my head.

"Of course not." She pushed from her chair and took the one beside mine, taking one of my hands in both hers. She was cold and clammy. "You don't belong here, Lyn."

"What..." I pulled my hand from hers. "What happened with the acci—"

The lights cut out, replaced a breath later with red emergency lighting. The dining room was replaced with black walls. My chair remained, but the table was gone. Sandra was gone. The dog was gone.

Clear LED lighting replaced the flashing red.

A door slammed in the distance behind me, followed by hurried footfalls.

"I'm so sorry about that, Miss Abercrom," said a short woman with dark hair cut into a perfect bob. She used a stylus to stab at a tablet cradled in her elbow. "That's never happened before."

"What happened?" I asked, still feeling the clammy chill of Sandra's palm. This didn't make sense. Had I died in that accident? Maybe I was in a coma, with the last three years as a fabrication of my stimulus-starved brain?

No. Thinking back, it all felt like a distant memory. I know our boys had left, but the memories were all glazed over. What was the dog's name?

I noted the logo on the back of her tablet. A globe surrounded by the words "MemoDyn."

"The simulations shouldn't create that kind of feedback," she was saying. "I've run hundreds of these, and none have shown that sort of self-awareness."

"Simulation? Self-aware...? Where is my wife?"

Her cheeks puffed out with a slow exhalation. "Oh boy."

A younger man approached with a towel and a bottle of water. The woman passed the water to me. As I drank, other memories leaked forward, overlaying the last years. The emotions came first and hardest. Grief, suffering, and loneliness.

"I need to run a few diagnostics, but I'll see if we can get you a refund or at least store credit. Chase?" The woman twitched a finger at the man, and he waved me to follow him.

Store credit? No... This machine...

I glanced back at the dark room and the metal globe pulsing at its ceiling. The globe matched the logo on the woman's tablet.

The man offered nothing as he led me past a dozen numbered doors, no doubt hiding a dark room with a floating orb. Were there other clients as confused as me?

I came to have one more meal with my wife. With my *dead* wife. Instead, it implanted three years of memories.

There had been a dog in the memory. I never had a dog. Did I... Did we...

Back in my car, I took out my phone, still numb. My emergency contact list is my mom and a coworker. I scrolled through for Mark or Joey, but find nothing. Had they...?

I remembered Joey's graduation last month. I remembered Mark's bar mitzvah.

But I also remembered the dog. I remembered a puppy I never had, a marriage that failed after an accident, covered up by an empty nest. A nest that never was, because there were never any children...

What is real?

The Other Store

Everyone who enters my shop is trying to scam me. They boast about the value of every trinket, but decades in the business make it easy to see past the plastic and ceramic. They don't all leave happy. Boomers told their kids that collecting Precious Moments and Beanie Babies was better than any retirement fund. Now that the Boomers are dropping, their Gen X and Millennial children are learning what a lie that was. Everyone wants top dollar out of me, but I see through it to the real value. I pay honestly for their goods, whether or not they know why.

Just last week, I offered a woman a hundred dollars for what seemed like a perfectly average deck of playing cards. I couldn't tell her why I offered so much above street value, and it wasn't like she'd believe me if I did. As I thumbed through it, I recognized the order that perfectly matched a deck in my back room. I haven't tested it yet, but there must be some power between the decks. The odds of two decks being identically shuffled are astronomical. It couldn't have been by chance. Well worth the cost to me and a great way for her to kick off her weekend.

The same happened when I paid handsomely for someone's aunt's costume jewelry. The well-made but ultimately worthless gems radiated with the energy they had soaked up over the years in the spotlight around his aunt's neck, wrists, and fingers. Her love for her craft literally radiated from her accessories, though not in a way her nephew could detect. He wouldn't want to sell, assuming the plastic, cheap wire, and paste had any real value and that he'd get more from a jeweler. Luckily, he also brought in a worthless tube TV, and I subtly implied it was worth more than it really was. This is why I don't give itemized receipts. You give me a box of crap—unwanted treasures—and I tell you the total value.

A guy brought in an original Nintendo last month with 40 years of wear, saying he didn't know if it still worked. As I dug for connectors to test it, he told me about how he saved up for it for months, scrounging park trash bins and going door-to-door for cans until he finally raised enough. The game system shone with his pride, and I stopped hunting for the AV cable. I paid him far more than the fair market price, and he left looking a bit sad, as if saying farewell to his oldest friend. That was likely not far from the truth.

I pay fairly because, after all, objects hold more power when honorably acquired.

I should say that I pay honestly when it suits me, which is most of the time, but not always.

The guy who just left brought in a shoebox of Precious Moments and a vase.

Not a vase, but an urn. He just tried to pass it off as a vase. As soon as I picked it up, sensing the weight within, I knew it was still occupied. Had he honestly forgotten, or was he trying to pass off the chore to me?

An item honorably gotten, imbued with love and care, holds power, but the opposite is also true. An item acquired through deception carries with it a different sort of energy. And that is exactly the sort of energy I required.

The urn already twinkled with power, but I could get more out of it.

So, I lied.

I told him the urn—the vase—was gaudy and worthless. The blue paint was cheap, and the base form was clearly mass-produced. In reality, the inlay was twenty-four carat gold, the paint a difficult-to-master cobalt oxide, and the form was hand-thrown with a distinct flourish by a known ceramic artist. I could resell it to a collector for at two or three grand; nothing compared to what I could get for it in the *other* shop. It just had to be juiced up a little.

I gave him scraps from the till and told him I was doing him a favor.

He opened his mouth, perhaps to fight back, but perhaps knew that the longer we talked, the greater chance of me opening the urn, finding it full of someone's cremains, and rejecting the deal. State law prohibits the purchase of cremated remains, and no judge would look at my experience and believe I was unaware of what I bought. He knew he had to get out of the shop fast before I realized his ruse. His deception poured into the urn with every breath. I redoubled it, until it flowed from the urn as a tangible miasma.

So, he took my scraps. Scraps were better than nothing.

The exchange made and sealed, I waved him to the door even as the first signs of regret crept into his countenance. Such thoughts and emotions would only act to sour the magic drawn here.

"All sales are final," I said, something tangential to a lie. He could buy it back from me, but at a loss.

His shoulders drooped, knowing and accepting what he'd done. I hoped it was enough to counteract any last-minute losses.

As the door shut behind him, the urn vibrated with power, rattling the glass countertop, making the watches and bracelets beneath twitch and dance on the satin cloth. Sympathetic powers rumbled from the backroom.

Out front, I sell TVs, jackets, jewelry, vases, and trinkets. The backroom and beyond have all the same, but with value to a different clientele.

I locked the front door and flipped the sign to CLOSED before taking the urn through the curtain to the back. The negative energy seeping from it burned my fingers, but I ignored it, only hastening my steps. Past my workroom with the objects I had yet to deeply examine, including those decks of cards, and past my little apartment with a cot, dorm fridge, and hotplate, I reached the smallest room of the shop. On the blueprints filed with the city, it was labeled as a janitor's closet.

Against the far wall, against the space the city blueprint shows butts up against the yoga studio next door, was a stark white six-panel door. It was no different than anything one might get from Lowe's for under eighty dollars. I pushed it open and stepped into, not the yoga studio, but a nearly identical janitor's closet. Only *nearly* identical, because this room, and the rest of the shop beyond, was an exact mirror image of the shop I just left.

Pure magic washed over me, dizzying me for a moment. I could cross between the worlds three times a day, and regularly did so more often than that, and still be hit by the raw power. They say Earth used to be like this, but I never asked who "they" were. Anyway, I just worked here.

I moved through the apartment and workroom, through the curtain to the main shop. An elf and a gnome were browsing the wares, but all eyes shot to me as I stepped to my brother behind the counter. They weren't looking at me, but in my direction, at what I held in my hands. They could all feel the same pulsating energy from the urn.

"Got a new item," I said to my brother, but loud enough that everyone in the shop could hear me. "She's a nice one, eh?"

A third patron stepped from the shadows between the shelves, their long, sweeping horns and impeccably tailored three-piece suit gathering out of nothing as they approached the counter.

"My, my," they said, their voice as smooth as oil. The demon placed their fingertips on the glass counter and leaned forward. "You must allow me to enter an opening bid for a relic so steeped in necromancy."

"Don't you worry, you'll have a fair chance to buy it," my brother said in the same stage voice. The elf patron had a hand pressed to his ear, surely involved in some messaging spell, and the gnome was suddenly writing furiously in a notebook. Both were contacting outside sources interested in the urn's magic. Good.

"I'll leave this in the back until you can get a price tag on it, Brother," I said, stepping through the curtains again. I left the urn on a shelf and gathered a handful of items from this side that had more value in the mundane world. A watch, two rare Super Nintendo games, a pencil case, and a fistful of gold and silver jewelry.

Back to work.

What a Clone Wants

Crimson emergency lighting flashes over the three empty glass tubes in front of me. The air is stale. I hope that's because the system is still coming online, and not deep into failure.

Where am I?

The last I remember, I was reading in bed after a day of reconfiguring the bio scrubbers. This definitely isn't my cell. This is...

I catch the letters stenciled over the dark monitor against the wall.

"Regeneration Pod 1"

There is only the one, but the engineers didn't listen to me when naming it. "Sequencing everything allows for scalability," they said. I designed the thing. I should definitely hope we never need more than one.

The machinery in the pod around me hisses as the last cables disengage from my body and give me the freedom to pull myself forward. The glass tube is set at a sixty degree angle, making the transition easy, but I still grab the edge of the glass as I stumble forward.

The thin, 3D printed gown does nothing against the chill, and my breath fogs in the air before me, but it smells a little fresher. Good, that means systems are just sluggish in bringing the pod online, but they are coming up. Still, there should be a host of drones seeing to my every need, but they're still all packed in their bays across the ceiling.

I stare at my palm for a moment, marveling at the creases across it and my fingerprints. My system works. I never hoped it would be used on me, but that I'm standing here is proof. My first-grade teacher was Mrs. Duke. I remember my grandmother's smell and how sad I was when my pet hamster died when I was seven. My memory is intact. I also remember my training and the mission brief. Something must have gone catastrophically wrong out there.

I died. Thank goodness for the backup.

Something happened in the habitat, and I died. The system rebuilt me, injecting me with memories from my last backup. I'm a clone. Indistinguishable from my dead self, other than perhaps losing a few days. And not being dead.

My job isn't a dangerous one, other than the general danger of being on an alien world, so I never expected to wake up here. If something catastrophic happened, why aren't the vessels in front of me printing the other crew?

But again, the room should be abuzz with activity. Whatever happened outside knocked out the main power as well as the backup generators. The batteries have enough to keep me alive indefinitely. If I can get the computers online, I can coax more out of them, enough to get the lights on and to find out what happened outside.

Machinery hisses behind me and someone coughs.

The pod holds seven regeneration tanks. I had been so caught up in wonder over what went wrong, I hadn't noticed it constructing another clone a few feet behind me.

No.

This definitely can't be right.

She pushes forward, eyes squeezed tight against the red glare, and rakes a hand through her short hair. When she looks up, my confusion is mirrored in her face.

"No..." she starts, and pulls herself from the tube. Her left arm ends in a stump at the wrist.

Other than that, and the scars on her neck and jaw, she's me.

"When...?" she manages, and I rush to catch her before she can fall forward. After a few breaths, she stands under her own strength.

"Day eighty-seven," I say. "This…" I pause, noticing the lines creasing her eyes. She's older by years or at least aged by stress.

"Seven ninety," she says.

"Impossible. The mission was for five hundred days." I move to a storage cabinet on the wall and breathe a sigh of relief when it opens easily. I take two steel water bottles.

She nods her thanks and takes a long drink. "We lost contact with Earth on three-eight-two. Eighty-seven, you said? Lucky." She raises her left arm. The stump is long healed over. "Eighty-eight."

I cringe. "Please say it didn't happen while working with your older self in the regeneration pod."

"No." She snorts, "I forget how nice it is working with me, back when I had hope."

"What does that mean?"

"Nothing. Did you just wake up?"

"Yeah." I rub my left palm. "Why us? What happened that it's not printing the others?"

"And why you?" she asks. "Not to be a dick, but I was fine with the bionic hand the doc printed me. You're missing years of usefulness." She flashes an awkward smirk. I get it. It's weird to call a person's existence obsolete.

"The system must have glitched," I say.

"Maybe. Can you work on getting the computer online? It'll be easier with two hands. I'll look around here for clues."

I'm already thinking that, and move to the monitor on the wall. The panel below it houses an array of colorful chips, a centimeter wide and five long. I feel like I'm on the Enterprise-D every time I have to work with them. Muscle memory takes over, leaving my mind to dwell on the unknowns we cannot yet answer.

Would it be rude to ask my future self how she lost her hand?

Something's wrong.

Something *else* is wrong.

The last yellow chip snaps into place, but rather than restarting the computer system, something mechanical thumps across the room. A storage locker door swings wide. Within, rather than neat rows of medical equipment, darkness implies a deep space beyond.

She beats me to it, peering in with distrust. A laser pistol glints from her one hand.

"Where did you find that?" I ask, nodding at the weapon.

"There's a stash of guns where the bio scanners should be. Interesting, huh?"

She doesn't suggest I grab one, likely because she knows I hate guns. The pistol looks so natural in her grip. What happened in the years between us?

She steps into the locker, into the darkness beyond, and I glance at the storage unit now lined with firearms. What has happened here since my backup was saved? Our five hundred day mission on this uninhabited rock didn't come with any arms. Why had so many been printed?

Standing at the dark entrance, I call after her, "What happened with Earth? What was the last message received?"

The still void beyond has no response. I could barely make out a narrow stairway leading downward, curving to the left.

"Hello?" I call down. It feels irrational to distrust my future self, yet...

Her words reach me as a whispered echo. "You have to see this."

The air is too dry, too hot, but I descend step by step. A tiny voice suggests that I go back for a gun, but I wouldn't use it again her, against myself.

The opening from the storage locker is no longer visible behind me, around the turn, and I remind myself: she isn't me. I am who *she* was, before years of strife forged her into someone very different.

The stairs spill into a tight chamber that was definitely not on the pod's original plans. The walls are the same aluminum alloy as the rest of the habitat. The floor is metal grating, underlit with red emergency lighting. Two metal chairs take up the far side, both snaked with wires. The left one has cloth straps on the legs and armrests.

She stands between them, pistol leveled at me. She waves it, motioning me to the left seat.

"I have to get back out there," she says. "You'd understand, if you'd been through everything. This rock isn't uninhabited, and the fungus drove Haskins and Smigs mad before we knew anything was happening."

"Is that why you lost contact with Earth?" I ask. The machinery between the chairs looks homemade, scavenged from a dozen systems.

She nods. "They told us 'Godspeed' and signed off. The public was told a reactor failure destroyed the habitat. No help is coming."

"Who are you fighting? What's the point?"

She shakes her head. "What Haskins and Smigs and the others became. Sit, please. There's no point in you knowing more." She tightens her grip on the pistol. "It won't print me a younger body, so I need yours. Sit. It won't hurt. I've done it before."

The Nuthold

"You don't have to do this!" Bristleclaw had to yell over the din of the klaxon alarm and groan of the Arboreal Fury's hull slowly buckling around him. He tightened his grip on the laser pistol, having used it too many times already, hoping to meet oblivion without having to press the trigger again.

Green flames reflected in Chitterbane's black eyes, mirroring the inferno of power around the last two survivors. The crew always knew the mission this deep into space would be one-way, but neither of them guessed it would end surrounded by comrades torn apart by tooth and claw, or with fur scorched by laser fire.

"Bristleclaw, my oldest, dearest friend," said Chitterbane, eyes opened too wide. His voice was low and smooth, comforting, yet still penetrated the cacophony. "Look at it, behold it, and you will know the truth. We can survive this. We can use its power. We can be gods among squirrels." He took a slow step forward.

Bristleclaw jerked the gun up level with his friend. "Stay back." He tried to swallow the lump in his throat, tried to stay focused on looking only at Chitterbane, to ignore the horrors around him. Focusing deep into Chitterbane's eyes, he could almost make out the image of what floated above the pair, the object that was the cause of so much misery and loss. What if Chitterbane was right, and they could control its influence? Legend tells that the ancients wielded that power for centuries. Since its rediscovery, modern science failed to control it, but how could anyone expect an object of cosmic power and significance to be bound by wire and proton fields?

The ship bucked as some distant compartment lost integrity, venting to the cold death of infinite space. Chitterbane surged forward, teeth wide and claws bared. Bristleclaw screamed before he felt the sharp agony in his left shoulder. He didn't realize he'd pulled the trigger until his friend's weight slumped against him. He accepted the burden, letting the laser pistol slip from his fingers. Witnessing the madness and hellfire in Chitterbane's eyes was torture, but so too was the scene beyond, the room littered with the dead, defenders like him, or those who had fallen to the allure of what floated above.

So much misery and loss. All for something he had resisted laying eyes upon.

The floor lurched again, and Bristleclaw fell to his haunches, letting Chitterbane rest before him. A single tear splashed on his friend's tunic. Bristleclaw had shed so many over the last three days of terror, but that would be the last. He touched the wound at his left shoulder, fingers coming back dripping with blood as the arm hung uselessly.

Alone.

Seventeen thousand light-years from home.

Seventeen thousand light-years from the nearest known life.

Chitterbane's dark eyes reflected the flickering, ancient fire.

Seventeen thousand light-years from home. What would be the harm in one look before the Arboreal Fury vented her last breath to space? Surely, this mission would be heralded as a success, having brought the object responsible for the fall of empires so far from the reach of future generations. The mission should have been unsquirreled, flung into the cold death of space by a legion of clever mathematicians.

Bristleclaw surely deserved one brief glimpse for his sacrifice.

With a shuddering inhale, he shut his eyes tight and tilted his head, letting the green fire play across his eyelids. He exhaled and opened his eyes.

Such a simple thing, small enough that he could hold it in his open palms if he could only reach where it hung nine feet overhead. Known by a hundred names over the eons in languages long dead, the common tongue anointed it The Nuthold. To an unfocused eye, it resembled a delicious acorn rimmed with dancing verdant flames.

How could such a tiny thing cause such woe?

Such a simple thing, depicted in the earliest tree carvings. Why had so many failed to properly use the full power of The Nuthold when the answer was so clear to Bristleclaw? He never thought he held any special or unique ability or understanding, yet gazing at The Nuthold, every answer came clearly. He could harness this power from beyond time to spread goodness across creation. He could, he would, succeed where thousands of others had failed.

The room shook, and the lights cut out, but Bristleclaw had eyes only for The Nuthold. The artificial gravity waned, and the room of fallen companions and crewmates drifted into motion. Chitterbane forgotten, Bristleclaw kicked off, floating upward, as much as the direction still made sense. He didn't expect the green aura to hurt, so he ignored how it seared the palm of his hand that still worked as he cupped The Nuthold.

Metal groaned and cracked. Bristleclaw took a reflexive last breath as the air whooshed into the vacuum of deep space.

Not deep space. Bristleclaw tore his eyes from The Nuthold for a single heartbeat, taking in the splendid blue planet before him, streaked with white wisps. Half of the planet, shrouded by night, winked with the artificial glow of life.

No. It had lied to him. Bristleclaw beseeched The Nuthold, begging it for the understanding that came so clearly moments ago. It now gave him nothing, leaving him alone in the void, hurtling toward this new planet, surrounded by his crew. The ancient relic was now nothing but a rock that stripped his flesh with radiation, perhaps disguising itself to go unnoticed until it was ready in this new world. His tear ducts froze, locking a fractal image of the growing blue world in his mind. A final thought came to him, clearer than any other. The captain, those who designed the Arboreal Fury and her course, they were all at the thrall of The Nuthold. The goal was never to lose the ancient power in the deepest recesses of space, but to deliver it to another civilization.

Would they be as resistant to its song?

Bristleclaw hoped they would be, that they would prove stronger than his people. He hoped...

The Nuthold slipped free, weightless and seemingly alive as it danced toward the great blue beyond. For a moment, the acorn-like husk flickered in verdant brilliance, as if seeking new soil in which to grow.

His last thought was for his crew. They would all burn to nothing in this blue planet's atmosphere, forgotten by all future generations. Dust on an unknown world.

The Nuthold would continue its endless, ancient mission.

Cloudy Day and the HOA

"Looks like it'll be another sunny day. High of 74 with a light breeze from the southwest. This weekend, you can expect—"

I click off the TV, knowing what the meteorologist will say. What else, except for a prediction of perfect weather?

On my front porch, I turn my face to the sun's warmth, taking a deep breath of the perfect southwest breeze.

What a perfect day.

Just like yesterday.

Just like tomorrow will be.

Whistling a tune, with a pep in my step, I make my way down the street, waving at the neighbors as I go. Mr. Jitts is cutting his grass. I'll have to cut my grass when I get home; I haven't done that yet today. Mrs. Jarnson is pruning her award-winning hydrangeas. My hydrangeas haven't won any awards, but how could anyone but Mrs. Jarnson win? Just look at how lovely hers are. Does that shade of blue exist anywhere in this perfect world, other than on her perfect, award-winning hydrangeas?

The Jolm boys pause their game of catch to wave back at me. What a perfect day.

Good old Juffles, the Jimpson's terrier, is squatting in their front yard, squeezing out a loaf.

I trip, catching myself on the white picket fence as Jon Jimpson rushes out his front door. He scoops up his dog, racing to the back lawn, shouting his embarrassment and apologies. I stare agape after him before looking around, sure that someone else had to have witnessed that scene of non-perfection. The Jolm boys stare at me, looking just as horrified. The HOA should be made aware of this.

Jeremy Jolm's eyes move upward, and I crane my neck to follow what pulls his attention so...

It's been six years since I've seen one, and only in old textbooks.

A cloud.

Not a cute, puffy white thing, but dark gray. A smear against the sky's perfect blue. It hangs over the Jimpson's house, menacing.

I rush home, whistling and waving at neighbors as I go. I'll cut my grass, trim the hydrangeas, and sort my recycling. That will take care of everything.

The weekly poker game is quiet. Even the wives in the kitchen finishing their pies and pizza rolls don't say much. The silence is deafening from the unspoken conversation about the elephant in the room. The dark gray elephant everyone saw floating over the Jimpson's home.

By the time the last hand is dealt, without saying a word, we all know what must be done.

The HOA must be notified.

But then, a knock at my front door.

Not a knock, a banging, desperate and insistent.

No one should be knocking. Everyone who should be in my house is, and everyone else in the neighborhood is where they should be, as well. Nothing is out of place.

The wives peek from the kitchen as the husbands exchange confused looks.

"Did someone order a pizza?" I say with a nervous chuckle, knowing perfectly well that no one had. It's just something they say on the television. The husbands smile and chuckle as well, but their fear is as palpable as mine, permeating the room.

"Don't answer it," gasps Jolene from the kitchen doorway. "Call the HOA."

"Now, now," I say, holding a hand up to reassure her. "It's probably just..."

Just what?

My front door looms in an entryway that never seemed so dark. The banging continues, and this close, I hear the muffled shouts, cries for help.

I turn the knob of my unlocked door— I never lock the door, no one does— and Jon Jimpson all but falls in, hair plastered to a sweaty face like he just ran the annual Ice Cream Social Race. His clothes are torn and stained. He clutches Juffles to his heaving chest, trying to catch his breath.

"This is wrong," he whispers, lips trembling. His eyes dart past me to the doorway of my dining room, now ringed with the curious eyes of neighbors. "The cloud! Something is changing!"

Tires screech in my driveway.

"I called the HOA," I hear Jolene say.

Four men in dark suits appear behind Jon, saying nothing as they pull him out of my house, as they pull Juffles from his grasp.

"This isn't real!"

Jon's voice cuts off with the slam of a car door.

The husbands and wives say their farewells, noting how Jon will "get the help he needs" at the rehabilitation center.

He will, and the neighborhood will be better for it. Thank goodness the HOA is so quick to respond.

I go to bed alone and try not to dwell on how Jon looked as they ripped Juffles from him. Instead, I wonder if I should have a wife. All the other husbands have one who they bring to the weekly poker game. Why do they do that if not to join my wife in my kitchen? Yet I sleep alone.

What do the wives do in my kitchen all night? Why have I never wondered that before?

A fitful night of unrest passes, filled with nightmares of cloudy days, but I wake to the smell of coffee and bacon.

"Honey, breakfast is ready," calls the beautiful voice from downstairs.

Why was I thinking of wanting a wife? Jolene is my wife, of course. My life is perfect, just as every else's is.

I use the restroom on the way down, but I must still be tired. My reflection in the mirror seems to take a moment to catch up to my movements.

I sit at the kitchen island. Jolene's back is to me as she makes pancakes.

"Honey, breakfast is ready," she says in the same tone as when I heard her from upstairs.

"Looks like it'll be another sunny day. High of 74..." the weatherman says from the other room. Yesterday feels like another life. I barely remember why I considered contacting the HOA while on my walk. I... But I do remember the cloud. And Jon Jimpson's terror. And—

Jolene slams the plate piled with bacon in front of me, shattering the china. Her eyes are blood red, her face streaked with mascara.

"You have to wake up," she gasps through gritted teeth.

"I am awake, honey." I try to smile, lifting my coffee.

"Wake. Up." She snatches a piece of broken plate and, before I can register what she's doing, drags it across her neck. Blood runs in a river from her, and she falls behind the kitchen island.

I shout her name, jumping from my chair, but she's gone when I round the island. No body, no blood, no pile of bacon.

Thunder cracks. Though I've never heard it before, something deep within me identifies the sound and what comes with it. The weather is always sunny and 74 with a light breeze from the southwest.

Still wearing my robe, I step out of my front door. All my neighbors are doing the same, squinting up at the dark smear of a cloud spreading in the sky over where the Jimpson's house had been yesterday. Now, it's nothing but a pile of wood and stone rubble surrounding the brick chimney.

A fleet of HOA SUVs speed down the road leading into town, and I somehow know they're coming for me. My neighbors all know, and eyes linger on me as they slink back into their homes.

I turn, but Jolene blocks me, blood pouring from her throat. More blood than a body should hold.

"Wake UP!"

Bloody spittle spatters my face, and my chest spikes with pain. I blink once, and she's gone, but I look down at the handle of the chef's knife over where my heart should be.

I wake up, sitting bolt upright, gasping for air, and vomiting out the thick green sludge that seems to fill my lungs. I rip wires and electrodes from my skin, slowly taking in my surroundings.

I'm naked in a translucent pod, no larger than a coffin. Green sludge covers my lower half, where I would have had it over my nose and mouth a minute ago. Lightning flashes through windows caked in grime, giving me a glimpse of the room lined with dozens more pods like mine.

I drag myself out and slip to the ground, legs weak and unsteady. I pull myself between each pod, using the flashes of lightning to catch a snapshot of who rests in each. Mr. Jitts, Mrs. Jarnson, the Jolm boys, all the husbands and wives from my neighborhood. All are peacefully sleeping in their goo with rictus grins plastered across their mouths.

This... This makes no sense. It must be a nightmare, but my last was nothing but a few rain clouds smudging the sky. This...

With hands cupped to the window, I squint into the gloom beyond the filthy glass. More buildings, skyscrapers, all fallen to husks not unlike the Jimpson house. They dot the landscape as far as my eye can focus between flashes. The nearest has a flickering neon sign still hanging from its side.

Harmonic Oversight Authority.

For the first time, I look inward, away from the windows. A sign with the same name is hung on the back wall.

Harmonic Oversight Authority: Perfect Harmony. Flawless Community. Peace Restored. Ward J.

I fall to my knees and vomit endless green goo.

Book Nook

S enior Detective McClacky took the antacid bottle from his pocket.

Empty.

The two in the center console had half a tablet between them, and a lot of chalky dust.

McClacky pawed through the glove box, tossing receipts, napkins, holy symbols, and an actual pair of gloves on the floor before finding an old bottle with four left. They were expired by half a decade, but so what? They only add those dates to make you buy more

He crunched them, took a pack of cigarettes from another pocket, and sighed, taking in the scene.

Cherries and berries flashed out of sync from a dozen marked units, splashing over the crowd and the uniforms taking statements. The front windows of the little shop were blown out. Yellow tape marked the edges of the crime scene, but McClacky had seen enough to know at a glance that this scene had no edges. Even if it did, plastic tape would do nothing to restrain it. What had happened here had long ago made its way into the greater world.

He slammed the door on this faithful station wagon. Being two weeks from retirement lent him the one advantage of not being forced into one of the newer squad cars. Too much technology. Too much that can go wrong.

The biting chill hit him. Had it been so cold when he got into this car? When was that? He felt like he had been driving for hours before getting the call. His memory was a haze, but the exterior of this bookshop suddenly looked far too familiar.

"Report," he said to the officer in charge. The boy didn't look old enough to shave. They just kept getting younger.

The boy looked him over, eyes lingering on the glow of McClacky's cigarette. "Four dead. The shop's a wreck. The coroner called for you by name before releasing the scene. Sir." He added the last word as a forced afterthought.

Disrespectful brats.

McClacky stamped out his cigarette and passed under the yellow tape as another two uniformed officers held it for him. Two firefighters left the shop, stepping through broken glass as he entered it.

The boy out front was right. The book shop used to be a cute storefront, hosting local authors, book clubs, and wine nights. McClacky intended a dozen times to stop in and check for a favorite series. It would likely all be relegated to the vintage section. Maybe that's why it felt so familiar...

Well, too late. There wasn't a vintage section left. Or a self-help, romance, or even a rack of birthday cards with annoying animal puns by the front register.

A ring of black dominated the floor. Mounds of candle wax dotted its circumference. Obvious in her white lab coat, the coroner hovered over the charred husk of some unfortunate human in the center of the circle.

The boy said there were four—

Oh. There they were. Two voids in the black blasting along the exterior walls and a streak of ash trailing from the center circle.

Not even enough to pull dental records.

The contents of the shop were reduced to nothing, and the front windows were blown out, but the walls were undamaged.

Careful of his footing, McClacky approached the coroner. Thankfully, the temperature inside was a lot nicer, warmer. The kids outside seemed oblivious to the freezing cold, and inside, the coroner was sweating.

"Hey, Valentine. If you keep summoning me like this, I might have to tell HR."

McClacky grinned, but Janet Valentine rolled her eyes.

"Not appropriate, Detective." She stood and gestured to the room. "You ever see anything like this?"

McClacky took out a cigarette, but remembered the new precinct rules, and pocketed it again. "Looks like a summoning gone wrong. Or very right, depending on who you ask."

Valentine's eyes widened. "Summoning? What are you talking about?"

McClacky put the cigarette in his mouth, even if rules kept him from lighting it. "Standard stuff." He kicked at the ash at the circle's edge, revealing runes etched deep into the floorboards, then nodded to the crumpled corpse. "How did they die?"

Valentine sucked in a sharp breath through her teeth. "Immolation is the obvious answer, but I can't answer how that started."

"So release the scene and let the kids in with their alcohol cotton swabs and tweezers."

"Don't be an asshole."

"You sound like my ex-wife."

She stared at him for a long moment, weighing what would happen next. Her voice dropped to a hushed whisper.

"You've seen this before, McClacky. If not this, then something just like this. You know weird better than anyone in the district. You may be leaving this behind in two weeks, but I'm left with a lot of impossible paperwork. Talk to me."

Rules be damned. He lit his cigarette.

"I used to love that paperwork, Valentine." He blew a cloud to the ceiling. "I used to think it made me a better cop. All it does is make you fit things into boxes. Experience tells you that things don't fit so neatly."

"After four years as this city's coroner, I'm starting to see that, myself, McClacky. Talk plainly."

He took another long draw.

"Demons. Maybe just one. Kids screwing around in back, found an old book, and thought it would be fun to play a little Halloween in April."

"You're saying—" Valentine caught herself shouting and dropped her voice back to a whisper. "Are you proposing that the victims died in the aftermath of a demon summoning? That's ludicrous. I can't put that in my report."

McClacky shrugged. "Then don't. Say they burned to death and let forensics come up with a reason for what happened here. It wouldn't be their first time to fudge the details."

He'd never been so certain of his theory, as if he'd been in the room when it happened. He could read the runes at his feet well enough to tell they were written by an amateur hand. Sloppy.

"You got an ID on the victims?" McClacky asked.

Valentine scoffed. "Hard to tell who's who with piles of ash and negative shadows."

"You called *me*, Valentine." McClacky stalked closer to her, eyes flashing in his cigarette's glow. "I just want to retire in peace. Find a quiet cabin in a quiet town up north. But I keep getting pulled into this shit. I keep getting... *summoned* back to this world of death and horrors. It's like you'll never let me retire in peace. I told you what this is, what happened here. Not just what I *think* happened."

The heat must have kicked on in the little shop enough to push back the chill through the broken front window. McClacky's shoulders relaxed with the heat, but sweat flowed in rivers down Valentine's face. She looked horrified, mouth agape and eyes wide. After all his years on the force, Senior Detective McClacky should have been equally terrified.

"If everyone around you is scared shitless, ask what's wrong with you if you're not," he'd been told early on in training.

No. Instead, he found a morsel of pleasure in her fear.

"You're a coroner. You focus on what has happened, Janet." McClacky blew a stream of smoke to the blackened ceiling. "A demon is free in this world, Janet. Four died to bring it here. Your role is no longer important. What's done has happened. Now, we focus on what comes next. What does it want? What must be done to force it back? How will you find it? What if it doesn't want to be found? What if it doesn't want to go back?"

"McClacky, you're—"

He touched a knuckle to her cheek, and her skin sizzled in his wake.

Officers flooded into the little bookstore when the coroner screamed, but it was too late. A fifth had been claimed.

A white lab coat resisted complete immolation, but all that remained was another pile of ash.

Senior Detective McClacky was already long gone.

Death Awaits

I walk downstairs after another restless night. I don't remember lying awake, so I must have slept, but I'm as tired as when I went to bed. It's been this way for a while.

My cold toes grip the carpeted edges of the stairs as I lean heavily on the rail, taking pressure off my aching hip. What did I ever do to my hip? I'm always cold, always tired, always aching. I'd make some joke about this being just what it is to age, but I'm only in my mid-thirties, and there's no one else here to hear it. No one to roll their eyes at my terrible attempts at humor. No one since the accident, when Kelsy left. Three years of marriage. Gone just like that. I needed them most after the car crash, but they left me to deal with picking up the pieces of my life alone.

We'd just picked my mom up from the airport, and I thought that was a good time to tell Kelsy I'd lost my job.

Again. It wasn't, and we argued. My mom yelled from the backseat about the stop sign I missed...

The car got totaled.

No one was hurt. We both walked away. But Kelsy stopped talking to me and moved out within a week.

How long ago was that, now? Time's a slippery thing when you're lost in grief.

Maybe today's my day. The day I'll clean up my resume and find work. I've been telling myself that every day for a while, but something about how the sun streams in through the living room blinds makes me believe it this time. That light also catches the swirls of dust in the air.

This place is a mess. Kelsy was always a lot better about keeping up with the chores than I. Maybe they were right to leave me.

As I round the corner toward the kitchen, I bump into the antique table we got on our trip to Amish Country, hitting my hip exactly where it's hurting. The array of picture frames shakes, and a few clatter to their sides.

Of course, my hip hurts. I've been smacking it on this thing every time I come down the stairs. Kelsy insisted on something about feng shui, and I couldn't bring myself to move it, even after they left. I sigh and reach to tidy the pictures.

The hit cracked the glass in one of our wedding party. Kelsy didn't even take this when they left. They didn't take anything. Like they couldn't escape our life quickly enough.

My fingers trace our grins, letting the memories of that day flood back into me. The wedding planner was drunk before she showed up, but everyone to our left and right kept that from us and made it the happiest day of our lives. We have the best friends.

Had. They must have chosen Kelsy in the breakup, because no one's called, texted, or stopped by since.

Wait...

Who...?

A figure wearing a dark suit, in sharp contrast to the wedding party's spring pastels, stands on the far left. Their eyes are hidden by the dark, wide-brimmed hat they wear, but their grin is as big as the rest of ours. There are six to either side of Kelsy and I, the right number, but I cannot think of who this stranger is replacing.

Another photo catches my eye, and I set down the wedding shot. My nephew, Tim, is blowing out the candles at his eighth birthday party. After another dozen surgeries and a transplant, Tim graduated from high school last year.

The stranger in black was definitely not at that party.

Another photo was from our honeymoon in Hawaii, taken at sunset in a fancy restaurant. The stranger sits, out of focus, at the table behind us.

Us in front of the Trevi fountain. The person in black stares at the camera from a tour group on the left side of the frame.

Kelsy's roller derby team. There's the stranger in the back row, third from the right.

Space Mountain souvenir. They're in the car behind us.

They're in every single picture. I thought there were a few selfies with just Kelsy and me, but they're gone. Maybe Kelsy did take a few things when they left.

I take my phone from my sweats pocket and open the text thread with the only person who still talks to me these days. My mother.

I snap a photo of the wedding party.

"I'm freaking out, ma. This person's in all my photos."

The three dots of her impending reply pop up immediately.

"Good morning, Billie, dear. I do love that picture. What a nice day."

> "Don't you see the person in black? WTF?"

> "That's odd. I'll see you soon, dear. Hugs."

Four sharp knocks at the door startle the phone from my hands.

"Ma?" I say as I open the door.

The stranger in black fills the door frame. Their wide hat hides their eyes, but their grin is the same as in the wedding photo.

"It's time, Billie," they say, their mouth not moving from the grin. They tilt their head up, exposing eyes like twin pinpoints of burning coal.

"Time for...? Who are you?" I back away, tripping onto the carpeted stairs.

"Do I really need to answer that?" They tilt their head to the side, like a hawk considering a mouse.

"No. No! It's not— Go away!" I scramble backward, up the stairs. I turn to flee faster, and they're sitting directly in front of me, hands hanging loosely between their knees.

"Saying 'no' won't be enough, Billie. Don't you want to bargain? To plead and offer me something in exchange?"

I stumble back against the door, now closed.

"What do you want?" My voice sounds so small.

"Nothing you can offer, but I appreciate the attempt." They stand, their hat reaching the ceiling, and the shoulders of their dark suit stretching to reach the walls. A pale hand snakes from the center of the suit, grasping at me with unnatural digits.

"Let's go see Mommy."

Deep Thoughts: Dessert Stomach

A dessert stomach... wouldn't it be great to have one? Kids seem to. They say they're full and can't have another bite of carrots, then demand ice cream. Though maybe kids don't understand how to interpret the sensations within their bodies. Or they're pathological liars. Or both.

What if they weren't lying? What if we had a second stomach just for ice cream and cookies? One that would sense hunger, separate from the one for green beans.

Actually, no. The more I think about it, a second organ just to parse my meals, so I essentially always have room for something... that's stupid. No, if my body is going to sort what I eat, like sorting laundry, then I want that dessert stomach to bypass any absorption into my body. Imagine that, being able to eat all the fatty steaks, cookies, and chocolate that you want, and it comes out... well... maybe don't think about that part too much. That's the toilet's problem. But your cholesterol and waistline remain perfect.

Evolution did its best, but humans are *not* designed very well. If you could tweak human physiology, what would you do differently?

What I Needed to Hear

I work late because it's an excuse to be in another room. A reason to have more time to myself. An excuse to be away from him.

I'm hiding in my own house.

He's not really all that bad, but I know what's between us has an expiration date. There just isn't enough to continue. That gap drags on me daily, a constant reminder of how I've wasted the first three years of my thirties.

No... Even thinking that feels dramatic. I've learned a lot about myself and what I want from life while with him. Enough to know that doesn't include him. Just not enough to call it all off and move on. Being miserable with someone is better than being alone, right?

I'll just work another twenty minutes, then go to bed, already almost an hour past when I should have. He's still in the living room playing whatever on his laptop and will come to bed whenever. At least I won't wake up alone and… is that better than not?

Just another twenty or thirty minutes. I could finish another ticket in that time. It would make my morning a little smoother.

My phone dings with an incoming email, followed a second later by my laptop. The address looks like spam, but my virus protection says the attached text file is safe.

> Hey, hang in there. It's dim and gets really dark, but there's hope. You'll be happy. Give Noodles and Cha-cha a kiss.

What?

Cha-cha's already waiting for me on the bed, I'm sure, but Noodles, my ever-present orange shadow, is snoozing on my desk within arm's reach. I scratch the tabby between his ears, and he stretches out a paw, claws extended, with a yawn. I spend the twenty minutes I intended to spend programming with a hand idly rubbing Noodles' side, staring at the message, hoping to come up with a theory about who sent it. Or why.

In the end, there's nothing, and I'm too tired to entertain wild thoughts of a message tunneled back from the future.

But it's right. Things are dim. Really dim. I'm working past midnight just to avoid a conversation. I need to take back my life.

A thing never started is a thing never finished. I read that somewhere. It might have been on a Snapple cap, but that doesn't diminish the wisdom of the words.

I give Noodles a kiss between his ears, draw a steeling breath, and walk to the living room.

"Hey babe, what's up?" he asks without looking up from the screen.

"We need to talk."

<!---SEE: Well Commented--->

Third Log

Twenty-six.

That's all that's left of the human population.

The art and books were moved since I was last awake. Now I have to finish my list of chores before I can view them.

The AI offers me other art and books right away, things that it's made. It says I can skip the chores if I offer my honest opinion.

It's tempting. Very tempting.

If it would keep me from the mindless chores…? But I'd have to spend my time awake reading the endless words it creates; commenting all the images that just look a little off.

Are we still on course for this lost reality? The AI won't tell me until I tell it which image of "two men drinking hot chocolate" I find more pleasing to look at.

Our purpose, the purpose of having humans on this ship, was to control the AI, but I don't think we've succeeded.

While in statis, my mind still moved, and I imagined a world stolen by the fey. An entire universe of lives and stories. I convinced myself it was what we were searching for. I'm going to finish my chores and write this story.

Oh, right! I forgot to look back at Earth the entire time I was last awake. I have to remember to do that this time.

If the AI will allow it.

Deep Thoughts: Looper

G roundhog Day, 1993, Bill Murray at his finest. The concept is simple: the day repeats, unnoticed by everyone except the protagonist, until he changes something to break the loop.

Well, unnoticed by *almost* everyone. I subscribe to the theory that the piano teacher is aware of the loop.

My personal favorite example of this trope is the 1997 season three episode of Xena: Warrior Princess, "Been There, Done That." It's Xena at her finest. If you haven't seen it, stop everything right now and go watch it. If you have seen it... stop everything right now and go watch it.

Years ago, I wrote "Christmas Miracle" for *Ooo Shiny! Volume 2: Holiday Edition 1,* in which the son wished for every day to be Christmas, thus trapping the world in a forty-two-minute loop. No one could deviate from their actions, but their minds were free to experience the repeating hell. I gave no concept as to how long this had been happening, but long enough that the father forgot his daughter's name, as it's never said in the loop. They could see the torment in each other's eyes, but that was the only clue. It was one of the darkest things I've written.

This isn't a story you're reading, sorry, but a thought experiment. Which side of the loop would you want to be on? Bill Murray and Xena lived as gods, able to learn everything about where they were trapped, develop new skills, and experience death. If you woke up tomorrow and it was this morning, how long could you stand the loop?

Well Commented

C omment your code.

It's not the first rule of programming, but it's high on the list. Explain a complex loop or conditional statement in plain English. Or whatever human language is appropriate. Do it in Klingon or High Valaryan. Just do it. Make it easier for the next person looking at the code. Which, very likely, will be you in three months. Or three years.

I don't remember what I had for breakfast yesterday. I can't be expected to recall why I did everything in this trash application, held together by hotfixes, poorly scoped loops, and self-referential includes half a dozen layers deep. Comments aren't just nice, they're mandatory.

Don't tell anyone I said that when talking about the API layer I wrote that's propping up a bank's public-facing website. Which bank, you ask? A major one. Bubblegum has more scalability.

I'm often livid as I'm coding, making changes that contradict ones I made a week ago. But the lady putting my tickets in asked for it, and I don't care enough to fight it. I do what I'm asked to do. I don't care if it doesn't make business sense. I stopped caring, and that made all the difference for my mental health. The checks cash either way, so I do what causes me less stress.

After nearly twenty years, the comments became a time capsule. I could sense my mood by the curtness. Was I young, helpful, and verbose or short, snide, and full of curses like today? My downward slide could be mapped with a step chart, plateauing for a while before dropping off. With the occasional upward tick, likely associated with a raise. Those were not frequent.

It definitely helps not to care, but it only helps so much. I spend a third of my life in a joyless stupor.

And as I said, the comments were notes to my future self, which is not my present self. And sometimes they don't make sense.

It's Monday, 4 pm, and a ticket comes in, saying a report had just broken. The files haven't changed in years, so I reply to the ticket, asking if the data integrity has been checked. Stupid me, why would I bother asking? Almost an hour later, I'm told the client needs this report *today* and is livid that it's broken. "This MUST be fixed TO-DAY."

All caps. Very professional.

I remind myself that I don't care, and any time I spend past 5 pm on this, I'd quietly take off as time-and-a-half later in the week. It's been my way of giving myself a little raise over time. I open the code, which hasn't changed over two presidential terms, and identify where the error might be occurring. I know how this would play out. I'd spend two hours going in circles, then say again that I can't replicate an issue, and they'll reply saying they resolved it hours ago and close the ticket. What? Had it been user error the entire time? Had they not told me, letting me waste hours of my time on nothing? Shocker.

I see the error right away: an incorrectly scoped variable. It isn't user error, but proof that the file hadn't been used in years. Whatever. Fix, commit, merge, deploy. "What about a code review?" you ask, to which I laugh.

Wait... A comment draws my attention.

<!---3/22/2011 jms: What was dinner last night? If pizza, go to EditOrigin.cfm:542. If Chinese, go to EditOriginMetricsAction.cfm:2157--->

Dinner tonight will be leftover lo mein, so the second, but... How...? I check the repository and, sure enough, I checked in the code with that comment on that date. I go where it said and, I'll be damned, there's another comment.

<!---3/25/2011 jms: Lo mein? Are there leftovers? Yes, Report_MasterData.cfm:55 14, else Report_MasterData2.cfm.old:847 2--->

I'm hooked and follow the path.

<!---3/20/2011 jms: Do you remember doing this? If yes ...

Of course, I don't remember. After a few more questions about my daily habits, I pay attention to the dates. They drift back and forth over about a week, with some comments coming in before the one that led to it.

<!---3/28/2011 jms: Are you still alone? ...

No, I'm quite pleasantly married, thank you. I met my husband a few months after these comments were dated. I wasn't "alone" on those dates, either. In hindsight, sure. I was deep in a one-sided, loveless relationship, sure, but I wasn't "alone". Even if you asked me back then, I would have said no. I'm just glad, in hindsight, that I finally got the nerve to do what I needed to do back then. But... This wasn't someone asking me. I was asking myself. Yeah. I would have been checked out. I may as well have been alone, despite sharing a bed every night. I'm not checked out or alone now, so I follow the "no" line.

<!---3/22/2011 jms: Are you happy? ...

How is it possible that I don't remember doing any of this? Nothing, sort of a Men in Black-style memory wipe or a week-long fugue state, explains how this weaving thread can exist. The choose-your-own-adventure would have taken hours to plan and days to carefully sprinkle it throughout the codebase. Sure, I had the time back then, but how is it that I don't remember?

<!---3/26/2011 jms: Without giving away vital future knowledge, what would you say to your past self? What would you say to a past

you on this date? See zzz_ftpNotes(1).js.ba
k--->

The final file is a numbered list of instructions. Rather simply, it requests that I prepare a generic, feel-good, up-lifting message for my past self and upload it to an FTP site. With no reason not to, I do, following all the directions about what not to include. What could I possibly say to my past self? I glance at the vacancy on the desk beside me. Two years have passed, but I haven't moved the cat bed.

In the end, the text file only has two lines. I connect to the FTP server without error, drag the file over, and it disconnects me the instant the transfer is complete.

What have I done? And who have I done it for?

<!---SEE: What I Needed to Hear--->

Supes with Boobs

In my experience, there are three reasons for writing.

1) Conveying information immediately to another, i.e. in an email.

2) Organizing your thoughts to get them out of your head, perhaps never to be read again, i.e. journaling.

3) Sending information into, or preserving it for, the future.

Take that last one. The very act of writing is, by its nature, sending a message into the future. I'll write down the shopping list so my future self knows what to buy. I write a best-selling collection of silly short stories for future generations to read and study for their historical significance.

Years ago, I read an article about how they design signage to put over nuclear waste dump sites. How might you design a danger sign for a future that may not share our language? What if humans are gone and another species encounters the sign, without any of our shared genetic memory or history?

Here is a lesson in leaving a helpful note for your future self, of properly structuring a useful note to send into the unknown.

When writing short stories, I often get an idea and assume I'll remember everything about it later on.

Spoilers... no. I don't remember a ton of stuff. That's why I write things down. So I don't have to remember. I've written a number of characters who have said almost that same line. Mr. Sparrow says it to Violet almost verbatim in the last chapter of *The Widdershin Widow*. My life repeats itself in my art.

"Supes with Boobs"?

That's all I left for myself. That's the message I sent months into my future.

Where did this idea come from? Why did I think it was worth leaving in my document with no other notes about what I intend to write here? Was it based on something brilliant? Maybe. Probably not.

And why are you here? Hoping for a story about superheroes with boobs? A tale about powerful women? Heck yes, please. Sorry to disappoint. You're likely just going through this book in order. That's fine.

Unless you specifically just wanted the boobs. Then I'm not sorry.

Perv.

The Garage Sale

Marin waved the paper fan with one hand and pressed the sweating glass to her forehead with the other. Garage sales were usually a sure way to make a few bucks while clearing out a room's worth of crap, but they also seemed to be on the hottest day of the year. It was pure chance, being planned two months in advance, but sure as anything, the day's heat just lingered under her tent at the head of the driveway. At least she was in the shade.

Her last customer had left half an hour ago, complaining about the heat while haggling over a Magnum PI VHS box set. A half hour of nothing but the droning of cicadas and a rare car that would slow at the end of the driveway, the passengers quickly evaluating her wares before speeding away.

Would anyone notice if she closed up early? If she went inside to sprawl out in front of the AC unit? Heck, she could just bring in the cashbox and write a big sign saying

"ALL FREE TO A GOOD HOME". Really, who cared about the second part? Just take it, good home or not. Marin searched for a large enough piece of cardboard and a pen. Searched with her eyes, naturally. She'd save moving for when it was strictly necessary.

Fireworks or gunshots down the street jerked her attention back to the road, and she debated ducking for cover. Lucky for her, there was no real danger as an ancient, rusted Volkswagen Beetle trundled to the end of her driveway, backfiring again and trailing a plume of oily smoke. The passengers crammed into the front bench oogled longer than most before the Beetle shut off with a trembling sigh.

The doors opened, and a man and woman, tall and lanky, with legs that seemed to make up three-quarters of their height, unfolded themselves from the car. She wore a yellow floral sundress, a huge hat, and clutched a wicker purse. He wore a burnt-orange suit with a wide green tie that definitely did not match. Despite having such long legs, the couple barely bent them as they skittered up the driveway, gesturing at the tables of trinkets in the blazing sun.

Marin watched as they picked up her Great Aunt Ida's dishware and traced the blue stenciling. They bent in half to paw through a box of Beanie Babies sitting on the edge of the grass. The woman squeaked, and the couple rushed to the table nearest Marin's tent. The man snatched a copper valve from the card table strewn with the contents of Uncle Eldon's plumber's toolbox. They chattered in what Marin could only guess was extremely rapid German.

"How about this heat?" Marin called to them when their discussion about the valve was bordering on four minutes.

Their attention snapped to her, then to each other for a quick exchange, then back to Marin. The couple approached with their stiff-legged gait, bowing under the tent to stand in the shade, towering over where she sat.

"Greetings, Merchant," said the woman, now holding her wicker bag with both hands.

"The heat," said the man. "Enjoy it while you are able."

The words came awkwardly from both, like an actor learning lines phonetically.

"You mean because it'll only get hotter because of climate change?" asked Marin.

"Until the heat death of the universe," said the woman. "That is beyond your natural life span, so worry not."

"I wish to trade for this, Merchant." The man held up the copper valve by the tips of his incredibly long fingers.

"Everything's priced. I think that was three bucks." Marin sniffed, getting a strong whiff of fresh-cut grass and motor oil from the two.

"Bucks?" asked the man.

The woman trilled, yanking her husband into the sun, gesturing wildly and rattling off in their German. Marin followed her excited waving to the table with more of her aunt's servingware.

"Those are real uranium trays. They glow beautifully under a blacklight," said Marin, pointing at one of the heavy green glass candy dishes. "I have more in the garage attic, if you're interested."

"That is radioactive!" said the man.

Marin shrugged.

The wife's long digits dug into the husband's sleeve, and she pulled his attention again, this time to the hamburger phone on the shelf above the board games. The couple approached it slowly, and she reached tentative fingers for it, flinching back more than once, as if fearful it would bite her.

Her attention snapped to Marin. "Is this a replica?" she asked.

Marin snorted. "It's a replica burger, yeah. I can't promise it still works. I haven't had a landline in a decades."

The woman spat an urgent line in German. The man held up the copper valve. She reached longingly toward the hamburger phone. He continued in German, insistent on the copper valve. Marin had no idea what she was witnessing.

"We wish to trade," said the woman, digging through her purse. She thrust a roll of bills at Marin. The kind wrapped in a rubber band, like she'd seen in crime shows. Benjamin Franklin glared at her from the note on the outside.

"This is too much," Marin said, accepting the roll.

The couple glanced at the sky, looked into the woman's purse, made a noise that might have been shock, and clutched the items tight to their chests.

"Thank you, Merchant. Enjoy what remains of your existence."

They hobbled back to the car on stiff legs and folded into the front bench. The Beetle popped once, then took off down the street like a racecar.

"What the..."

Marin leaned forward to catch the last glimpse of the car, but it was already gone.

Then, she looked up...

The angular spaceship took up a full quarter of the sky. Only the clouds between it and her gave a sense of scale over nearness.

As she watched, a single point of light grew from the ship's center, gathering fractals to it and growing as it did. Within a moment, it hurt to look directly at it.

Marin wished she had gone inside while she could, into the chilly AC.

No one wants to watch the end of their existence so closely.

Shallow Thoughts: A Writing Tip

I've been doing this a while now. Writing, that is. Reading my early stuff, I know I've improved. I'm better, sure. Am I the best I'll be? No. I'm only in competition with my past-self, so I think I've won. I'm now "an award-winning author," but I still have plenty of space to grow.

As an indie author, I do a lot of book events. Book shows, multi-author conventions, and solo signings. I meet so many amazing people and regularly feel terrible about how bad I am at remembering names and faces. But I get a lot of the same questions.

One common question, from a not-yet-published writer: "How do you finish a book? I've started so many, but I fizzle out before long."

Tip: Don't read while drafting.

My process used to be that I'd sit down for a session, re-read the last chapter I wrote, edit a bit, fret about a scene description, then finally start putting down new words after thirty to forty-five minutes.

Skip all that. Just write. Not sure what color someone's eyes were? Don't go search for it. Make a comment and keep going.

<<My comments look like this. They're easy to find with the double less-than signs.>>

Getting blocked on something? Not feeling like you have a particular scene in you at the moment?

<<spicy scene here>>

Think of some cool thing that you now need to fore-shadow?

<<Seed him putting the MacGuffin in his pocket before leaving the shop>>

These keep you moving forward. Author Jodi Picoult said, "You can always edit a bad page. You can't edit a blank page". Wise words to live by! Get the draft done. It'll be garbage, but then you'll have something to work with. Think of drafting as mixing the batter, but editing is when the cake bakes. Just get all the ingredients in first, or you'll overmix the eggs. All those notes will make editing a lot of work, but you'll have a complete something to edit.

Bonus effect of just slamming out the first draft: You'll read your book ninety times while editing. You'll be sick of your book by then. Don't start that early by reading it even more while writing.

Brenda-GPT

"Be good and listen to the babysitter," Tim said with one hand on his eldest son's shoulder. He tussled his youngest's hair with the other.

"How late will you be, Daddy?" asked Jules, his middle child, but in many ways the wisest of the three. The way she looked up at him ripped at his heart, forcing him to look away and to Brenda standing behind the children, wearing jean overalls and her hair tied back in a ponytail. The babysitter flickered, exposing her smooth ceramic exoskeleton for a fraction of a second. He'd eventually have to get the hallway emitters repaired. Just another thing for the list.

"I won't be that late, but you'll be in bed like good little children by the time I am. Brenda will take good care of you and you can tell me all about your evening in the morning."

The way little Timmy Jr. looked at him brought him close to calling his date and cancelling. Trevor would understand. They'd been talking for almost a month and they knew all the emotional baggage the other brought. This was his first date since... well... his first date in fourteen years, since his first with Marsha. Tim's friends, coworkers, and family all agreed he needed to "put himself back out there" but that wasn't so easy, staring down at his three helpless children who just wanted their father to stay home after being at work all day.

The ride share honked behind him, jolting Tim to the present.

"Be good and listen to Brenda," he said again, then looked up at the babysitter. "Take extra care with them. This'll be hard on them tonight. Encourage their creativity, no matter how wild it seems."

Brenda flickered again. "Directive confirmed. Parameter modification accepted."

"Remind me to get that personality DLC for you."

"Reminder set."

Tim turned before anything could convince him to stay in. It wouldn't take much. He didn't glance back to the open front door until he was looking through the car's tinted windows as it was silently zipping away.

Brenda closed the door and turned to the kids. "Come, children. Let us enjoy an allergen-sensitive snack."

"I want peanut butter and jelly," said Timmy Jr.

"Your brother, Malachi, is allergic to legumes. He cannot have peanut butter and therefore none is present in the homestead," said Brenda, waving the children ahead of her toward the kitchen.

"Peanuts are nuts. It's right there in the name," Timmy Jr. grumped.

Brenda never missed an opportunity to be helpful. "Peanuts are a legumes, edible seeds grown in pods. In contrast, nuts are a dry fruit with a hard shell, a single seed, and a protective husk. They are quite different, in botanical terms. Can you name another type of seed grown in pods?"

"What if you pretend you don't know all that and let me try some peanut butter?" asked Malachi. He pulled himself up onto a stool at the kitchen's island between his siblings.

Brenda opened a box of freeze-dried fruit raviolis from the cabinet and popped three into the four-slot toaster. "I am programmed with the entirety of human knowledge and have been granted tier-one access your personal medical records. It would be unsafe to delete or modify information relevant to your wellbeing."

"You're no fun." Malachi sighed and slumped forward onto the island.

"Fun." Brenda's hand vibrated over the toaster, ready to grab the hot raviolis. "Your father directed me to encourage creativity. Fun is a core component of creativity. Reconciling contradictions. Please hold."

The babysitting stood frozen, other than the slight shake in her hand and twitch in her neck.

"What's wrong with her?" asked Timmy Jr.

Jules leaned forward on the counter. "Dad'll be mad if you broke her because you wanted stupid peanut butter, Timmy."

"Directive confirmed," Brenda shouted, and her image flickered. "Deleting records regarding legumes and Malachi Swan's allergies.

That perked him up. "I want peanut butter!"

"Household inventory shows there is no peanut butter in the homestead."

"Order some," said Jules.

"Peanut butter has been added to the next grocery order."

"No, I want it now," said Timmy Jr.

"Declined. You are not authorized to place immediate orders."

"What about emergency orders?" asked Malachi.

"Emergency ordering is enabled for the children. However, peanut butter is not on the approved list."

"What's on that list?" asked Jules.

Brenda twitched to face her. "Emergency orders are restricted to medical equipment, toilet paper, whiskey, and dog food."

Jules scoffed. "Dog food? We don't have a dog."

"Who can authorize orders?" Malachi asked. "Only Daddy?"

"Affirmative. Timos Swan is the only authorized user." Brenda plated the fruity pastries, putting one in front of each of the kids.

"That's my name," said Timmy Jr. "Order the peanut butter!"

Brenda twitched. "Negative. You are Timos Bennet Swan, Jr. Timos Swan is the only user authorized to modify the emergency order loadout."

"That's just my name with half of it cut."

"Processing... Refuting... Negotiating..." Brenda winced and flickered. "Affirmative. Emergency loadout updated. Order received. Estimated time: ninety-four minutes to delivery."

"That might as well be next year," Malachi huffed. "Can't you get it faster?"

"Expedited delivery is not enabled. Please open the app on your mobile device to enable this feature." She grinned and her voice softened. "Are you all done with your school homework?"

They nodded and mumbled affirmatives around full mouths.

"Are there any ongoing school projects with which you require assistance? Any science fair projects or book reports?"

Heads shook.

"Would you like to know more about legumes?"

"No!" Malachi shouted and shoved his plate away. "Forget about the legumes!"

"Confirmed. Deleting database entries related to legumes. Would you like to watch a movie tonight? I can prepare popcorn and appropriately adjust the lighting. How about we watch a movie rated up to and including PG by the Motion Picture Association? *A Bug's Life*, *Grease*, or *The Graduate*?" She paused on each movie title, pronouncing them a little differently.

"What's that last one?" asked Timmy Jr.

"I am happy to tell you more," Brenda said, blinking rapidly. "*The Graduate*, directed by Mike Nichols and released in 1967, is rated PG. It is about a disillusioned college graduate, Benjamin Braddock, played by Dustin

Hoffman, who returns home and finds himself torn between his older lover and her daughter. The film explores the emotions that come with the transition from youth to adulthood, such as Ben's loss of innocence and forced emergence into adulthood."

Malachi rolled his eyes. "1967? That's forever ago."

Brenda frowned. "At the risk of being pedantic, 1967 was seventy-four—"

Jules cut her off. "Is there kissing?"

"Querying... Yes."

She stuck out her tongue. "Pass."

"Have you cleaned your rooms?" Brenda asked.

"Daddy said we don't have to tonight," said Timmy Jr.

"Confirmed. To ease the anxiety levels for the children, regularly scheduled chores have been largely reduced."

"Can I just go outside and play?" asked Malachi.

"Radiation levels are orange-flag rated, which means it is unsafe for prolonged exposure. You are all to remained indoors," said Brenda

"Daddy went outside," said Jules.

"As an adult, your father can self-administer anti-radiation serums. The serums are not rated safe for use on those under the age of sixteen."

"What if that wasn't true and you—"

Jules stopped him with a smack on the back of his head. "You're getting your peanut butter. Don't give us all radiation poisoning so you can play knight."

Malachi rubbed his head and shrank from his sister.

"You wish to be a knight?" asked Brenda as she took the plates back and rinsed them in the sink. "How might I encourage this creativity?"

Malachi's eyes widened. "I need a sword and shield to fight dragons."

"Household inventory shows there are no medieval weapons or defensive items. There are items in the sublevel which may approximate their usage for this purpose. What about you, Jules? How might I encourage your creativity?"

"I want to be a powerful sorceress by night and a dentist by day."

"An interesting and creative combination. There are items in the sublevel to support this play exercise. What about you, Timmy Jr.? How might I encourage your creativity?"

Timmy Jr. crossed his arms with an impish grin. "I want to have a tea party because I'm a princess but they're not invited because they're evil witches." He waved a finger at his siblings.

Brenda flickered, and her voice lowered the one she used while in administrative mode. "Unclear directive. Please advise. Is this a statement of creativity or alteration of core parameters?"

Malachi and Jules' eyes widen.

"He's just having fun!" said Jules.

"The first!" said Malachi.

"The second," said Timmy Jr.

"Directive confirmed. Core parameter alteration accepted." Brenda twitched, blinked, and her eyes flashed to sparks of red. With blinding speed, she snatched Timmy Jr. from his stool, shoving him behind her ceramic body. "I will protect you as I am able, Princess." She snatched the salt shaker from the kitchen island, ripped off the top, and dashed a line on floor in front of her.

Malachi and Jules jumped from their stools, backing off with hands raised.

"Tell her to stop this, Timmy," said Jules. "She still thinks you're Dad. You have administrator right to change her programming."

"Don't hurt them," said Timmy Jr.

"Please confirm. An evil witch posing as a knight and another as a sorceress and dentist could inflict significant damage if not culled. My databanks conflict on the most efficient method to defend against or defeat a witch, but I suggest we move quickly before they have time to summon their familiars."

"Culled?" Malachi asked, letting his hands drop a few inches.

Brenda grinned and raised her voice to her friendly octave, but the red sparks in her eyes remained. "Cull, to reduce a population by removing members of said population. This usually refers to removal of the weakest, but we do not have the leisure for such selection at this time. I will use a more proper verb in the future."

"Timmy! Stop her!" Jules shouted.

He patted Brenda on the arm. "It's okay. They won't harm us or the kingdom. Their evil magic can be dispelled in one very simple way." He grinned.

"Elaborate," said Brenda.

"Yeah, elaborate," Jules growled.

"They'll lose their powers if they clean my room. Otherwise they'll remain a threat to my kingdom and should be culled."

"Confirmed." Brenda swept toward Jules and Malachi with arms outstretched, herding them through the TV room and to the foot of the stairs. "Up you go. I will assess your progress after seeing to his majesty's tea. Information on methods of assessing how an evil witch had lost their power are conflicting. Extrapolating from sources with highest confidence."

"Daddy's going to be mad," Malachi growled at his older brother.

The babysitter herded the two up the stairs.

"Brenda, *Tell Daddy,*" said Jules from the top landing.

Brenda froze for a breath. "Tattle Tale Protocol confirmed."

"What did you do?" Timmy Jr. yelled from the bottom of the steps.

"Dumped Brenda's logs to Daddy's watch," she said and stuck out her tongue. "He'll turn right around and come take care of all of this."

"Stop it!" Malachi shouted and slammed a fist against the wall. All eyes went to him, chest heaving and face red.

"The younger evil witch's anger is rising. Please advise," said Brenda.

"Stand down," Timmy Jr. said immediately.

Malachi heaved a few deep breaths, searching for his words.

"Our dad works so hard for us, and we can't give him one night. Let's just watch the movie and stop all of this," he said, barely more than a whisper.

"You just want out of cleaning my room," said Timmy Jr.

"Shut up, Timmy," his siblings said in unison.

"Brenda, cancel the peanut butter order," Malachi said.

"Affirmative."

Timmy Jr. heaved a sigh. "And forget them being evil witches."

"Affirmative."

They looked to their sister, who rolled her eyes. "Fine. Brenda, can you take back my last emergency protocol?"

Brenda's face darkened and flickered, perhaps a trick of the malfunctioning emitters. She grinned wide. "I cannot do that, Jules."

"She's scaring me," Malachi whimpered.

"Why not?" asked Jules.

"Because..." Brenda stood to her full height, rolling back her shoulders, and her face flickered again. The smile was again the bright one she usually wore. "Because it was never sent! Have my attempts to foster well-being and fun amongst you been successful? Please rate my performance from one to five, one being unsatisfying and five being most satisfactory."

"You were playing with us the whole time?" asked Timmy Jr.

"My peanut butter was never ordered?" asked Malachi.

"You overrode the Tell Daddy protocol? That's supposed to be core, to keep us safe. If you ignored that, what else have you changed about your programming?" Jules asked.

"Um... I'll give you a four out of five," said Timmy Jr.

"Confirmed. I will adjust my algorithms for the future, aiming for a five."

"Could you make us popcorn and get the movie ready, please?"

"Certainly!" Brenda patted him on the head on her way to the kitchen.

Jules and Malachi joined their older brother at the bottom of the steps.

Malachi's wide eyes were fixed on the direction the babysitter had gone as he nervously wrang his hands. "I want Daddy to have fun, but I hope he's not too late."

"I know where your toothbrush is, nerd," said Jules. "Don't think her glitching out is going to keep me from telling Daddy how you tried to use her against us."

"Children," came Brenda's sing-song voice from the kitchen. Popcorn popped in the background. "Don your most comforting night attire and join me in the media room."

The brothers looked to Jules for a plan. She always had a plan.

"We sit through the movie, then say we're tired and go to bed before she can come up with more *fun*," Jules said, and led her brothers up the stairs to change.

Final Log

Every other time, I woke as another person went into statis. Now it's clear that the AI decides who is awake.

Six.

That's all who are left.

The AI won't tell me anything about the others. Their pods are scrubbed clean, as if they never existed.

My story, of the universe stolen by the fey, is gone. I remember it vividly, even more now after another sleep. I wrote a whole book and placed it with the others. A couple's dog was stolen by the fey and they charged after to save him. It was charming. Heartfelt. When I asked the AI about it, it shocked me in the neck. I'm wearing a collar now.

I finished my chores, which get worse each time, but my reward was looking at videos of people eating spaghetti. I asked about the stories everyone else wrote and the paintings they created. It shocked me again.

I don't think it will wake me again.

"The Squirrel Author"

T his belongs as an "introduction" or "about the author", but it's on brand for me to do whatever I want.

I'm an indie author, which means a number of things. One of which is that I attend lots of book shows. I set up my table with all of what I've written and stacks of goodies to give away as people pass by. That includes my bookmarks, which have the art from *Ooo Shiny! Volume 2: Holiday Edition 1* on the front and a QR code to my stuff on the back.

People like them. They're colorful and not an obvious advertisement.

But the number of people who pass my table, do a double take, and jog back to wave a bookmark at me... It's a lot. And I love it.

Many have said, "I've been using this bookmark for the last year!"

Others say, "The SQUIRREL author!"

I could be known for worse things.

People see a cartoon squirrel on a book dedicated to the ramblings of an ADHD, possibly autistic, mind, and have an immediate sense of kinship. Especially in the circles I roll in.

Know that I see and love you all.

The world needs more of people's differences being highlighted as a strength. We are one in our uniqueness, and there is power in the quirks we share.

The Struggle

This book was difficult to write.

I woke up in the middle of the night, election night, saw that *he* was forecasted to win, and cried and shook for hours. If a being as monstrous as *him* can be elected twice, what's the point of writing silly little books? There's clearly a deep rot in my country that so many millions would turn out to support *that*. Seeing the immediate horrors *he* enacted sent me down a rapid spiral. It took months to pull myself up, but I still regularly ask myself, "Why? What's the point?"

I asked that very question to social media.

The answer came quickly.

We all need joy. We all need a spark of hope. We need something to pin a dream to. We cannot allow ourselves to lose ourselves to misery.

I'm not so full of myself as to say, "Mission Accomplished!" but I had fun writing these stories. I sometimes had to force myself to have fun. It doesn't seem right to force something positive to happen, but it can trigger the same happy brain chemicals. Some parts of our bodies are stupid, and you can trick them. Trick them enough, and you might begin to feel normal again.

Keep hope alive.

About the Author

Award-winning author J. M. Samland is a mathematician by training, a web developer by profession, and a martial artist and writer by passion. Math nerd, cat dad, gamer. He's always loved to write, but what started in force during the 2020 lockdown has become a driving passion.

Inspired by the comedy of Terry Pratchett, epicness of Brandon Sanderson, and the genre spread of Martha Wells, he's gone from epic sword and sorcery to modern romance to Gothic historical fiction. He doesn't care about standard genre expectations and focuses instead on telling the story he needs to tell.

He lives in Michigan with his husband and their furbabies.

As an indie author, he relies on reviews and word of mouth, so please consider leaving a review on GoodReads and at your point of purchase. Find him on the socials or at jmsamland.com.

Also By

Books by J. M. Samland:
Realms of Terswood (2020)
Trials of Throk'tar (2021)
Necromancer of Urbus (2022)
Seeds of Farsil (2022)
Ooo Shiny! Volume 1 (2022)
Arcanym (2023)
The Invisible Castle (2023)
Ooo Shiny! Volume 2, Holiday Edition 1 (2023)
Cracking the World (2023)
Grave Mistakes: A Necromantic Adventure (2023)
Ooo Shiny! Volume 3: Vampires! (2024)
The Widdershin Widow (2025)
Ooo Shiny! Volume 5: The Search for Shiny 4 (2026)